Kate on the Coast

by Pat Brisson

illustrations by Rick Brown

Bradbury Press New York

Maxwell Macmillan Canada Toronto
Maxwell Macmillan International
New York Oxford Singapore Sydney

Bradbury Press
Macmillan Publishing Company
866 Third Avenue
New York, NY 10022

Maxwell Macmillan Canada, Inc.
1200 Eglinton Avenue East
Suite 200
Don Mills, Ontario M3C 3N1

Macmillan Publishing Company is part of the Maxwell Communication Group of Companies.

First edition
Printed and bound in Hong Kong by South China Printing Company (1988) Ltd.
10 9 8 7 6 5 4 3 2 1

The text of this book is set in ITC Veljovic Medium.
Book design by Julie Quan and Cathy Bobak

LIBRARY OF CONGRESS CATALOGING-IN-PUBLICATION DATA
Brisson, Pat.
Kate on the coast / by Pat Brisson ; illustrations by Rick Brown.
– 1st ed.
p. cm.
Summary: Kate's letters to her best friend back home chronicle her family's move to the Pacific Northwest and their travels in Washington, Alaska, Canada, California, Oregon, and Hawaii.
ISBN 0-02-714341-4
[1. Travel – Fiction. 2. Northwest, Pacific – Fiction. 3. Letters – Fiction.] I. Brown, Rick, ill. II. Title.
PZ7.B78046Kaw 1992
[Fic] – dc20 91-17046

For my godchild, Kate Pianucci;
my college roommate, Lucy Tooper;
my niece, Joanna Maleski;
and for Zachary, my youngest son

—P.B.

For David and Andrew

—R.B.

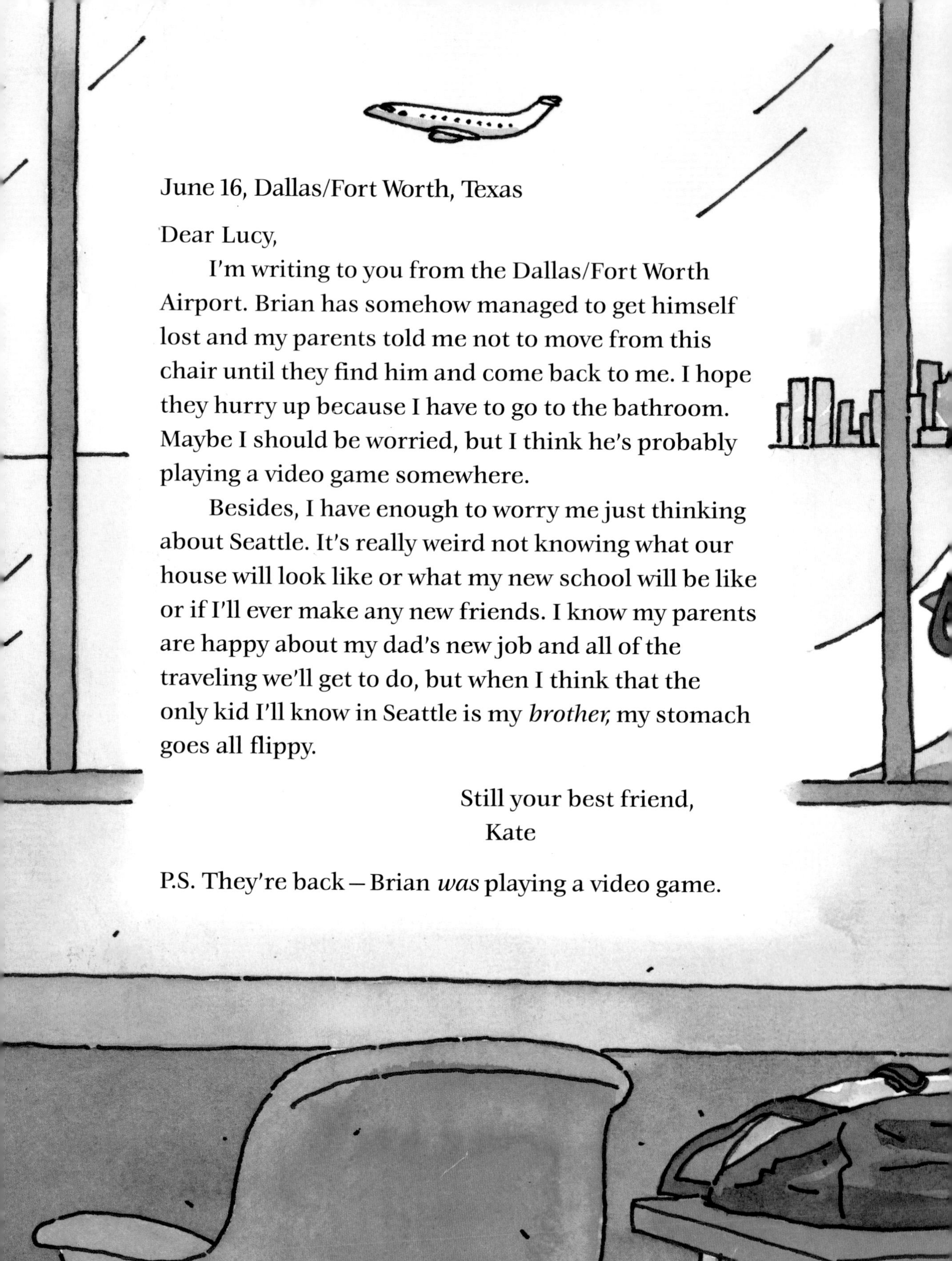

June 16, Dallas/Fort Worth, Texas

Dear Lucy,

I'm writing to you from the Dallas/Fort Worth Airport. Brian has somehow managed to get himself lost and my parents told me not to move from this chair until they find him and come back to me. I hope they hurry up because I have to go to the bathroom. Maybe I should be worried, but I think he's probably playing a video game somewhere.

Besides, I have enough to worry me just thinking about Seattle. It's really weird not knowing what our house will look like or what my new school will be like or if I'll ever make any new friends. I know my parents are happy about my dad's new job and all of the traveling we'll get to do, but when I think that the only kid I'll know in Seattle is my *brother,* my stomach goes all flippy.

Still your best friend,
Kate

P.S. They're back—Brian *was* playing a video game.

State Tree
Western
Hemlock

June 20, Seattle, Washington

Dear Lucy,

Washington is not like New Jersey. For one thing, you can see mountains with snow on them, even in the summer. The biggest one is Mount Rainier, and Dad says we'll take a drive up there one of these days. Brian thinks it will be great to have a snowball fight wearing shorts.

Another thing is that there's a monorail downtown. It was fun to ride on and look down at the people and buildings below. It reminded me of the time we rode the monorail at the Philadelphia Zoo. Do you remember when Bucko accidentally dropped his popcorn and it landed on a little kid in a stroller and the kid started to eat it? We rode on the monorail here when we went to the Space Needle, which is a really high tower with a lookout.

Our furniture has all been moved in, so my bedroom looks pretty much like it did in New Jersey, but I can't look out my window and see your house, so it's just not the same.

Still your best friend,
Kate

P.S. Buster and Bruno say hi!

State
Flower
Pink
Rhododendron

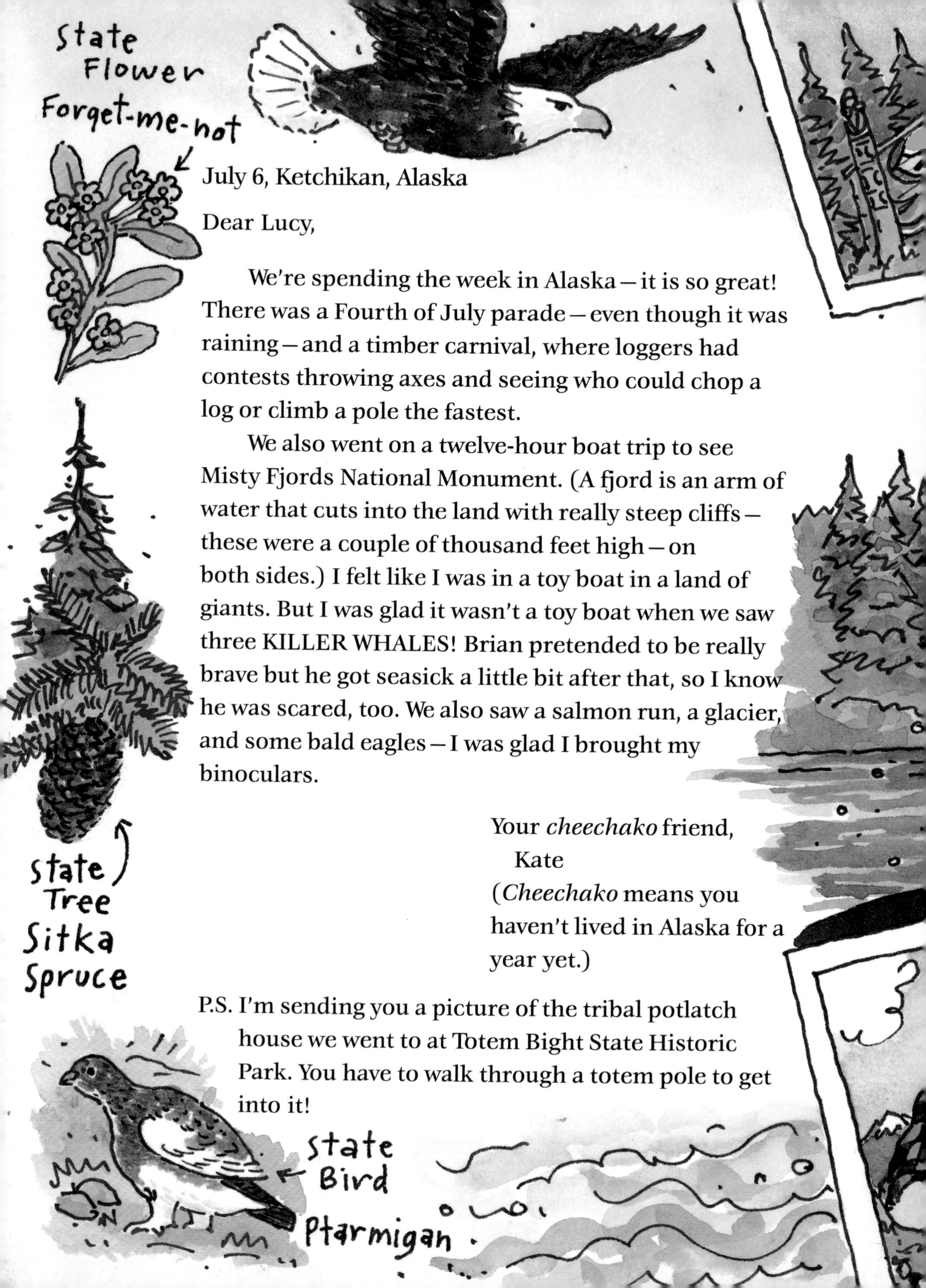

July 6, Ketchikan, Alaska

Dear Lucy,

We're spending the week in Alaska — it is so great! There was a Fourth of July parade — even though it was raining — and a timber carnival, where loggers had contests throwing axes and seeing who could chop a log or climb a pole the fastest.

We also went on a twelve-hour boat trip to see Misty Fjords National Monument. (A fjord is an arm of water that cuts into the land with really steep cliffs — these were a couple of thousand feet high — on both sides.) I felt like I was in a toy boat in a land of giants. But I was glad it wasn't a toy boat when we saw three KILLER WHALES! Brian pretended to be really brave but he got seasick a little bit after that, so I know he was scared, too. We also saw a salmon run, a glacier, and some bald eagles — I was glad I brought my binoculars.

Your *cheechako* friend,
Kate
(*Cheechako* means you haven't lived in Alaska for a year yet.)

P.S. I'm sending you a picture of the tribal potlatch house we went to at Totem Bight State Historic Park. You have to walk through a totem pole to get into it!

August 20, Seattle, Washington

Dear Lucy,

I'm writing to you at our picnic table by lantern light. The sky is moonless, black and filled with stars.

Do you remember when Mrs. Snyder showed us that movie about volcanoes and there were pictures of Mount Saint Helens with all the trees knocked down? We're camping for the weekend and we saw Mount Saint Helens for real today. We even went on a hike where we could actually see into the crater. And tonight there was a campfire, and a forest interpreter told stories and sang songs.

School starts soon and my mother said I'll probably make lots of new friends, but I wish I was back in New Jersey with you and Bucko. Do you think you could ever come out to visit?

Still your best friend,
Kate

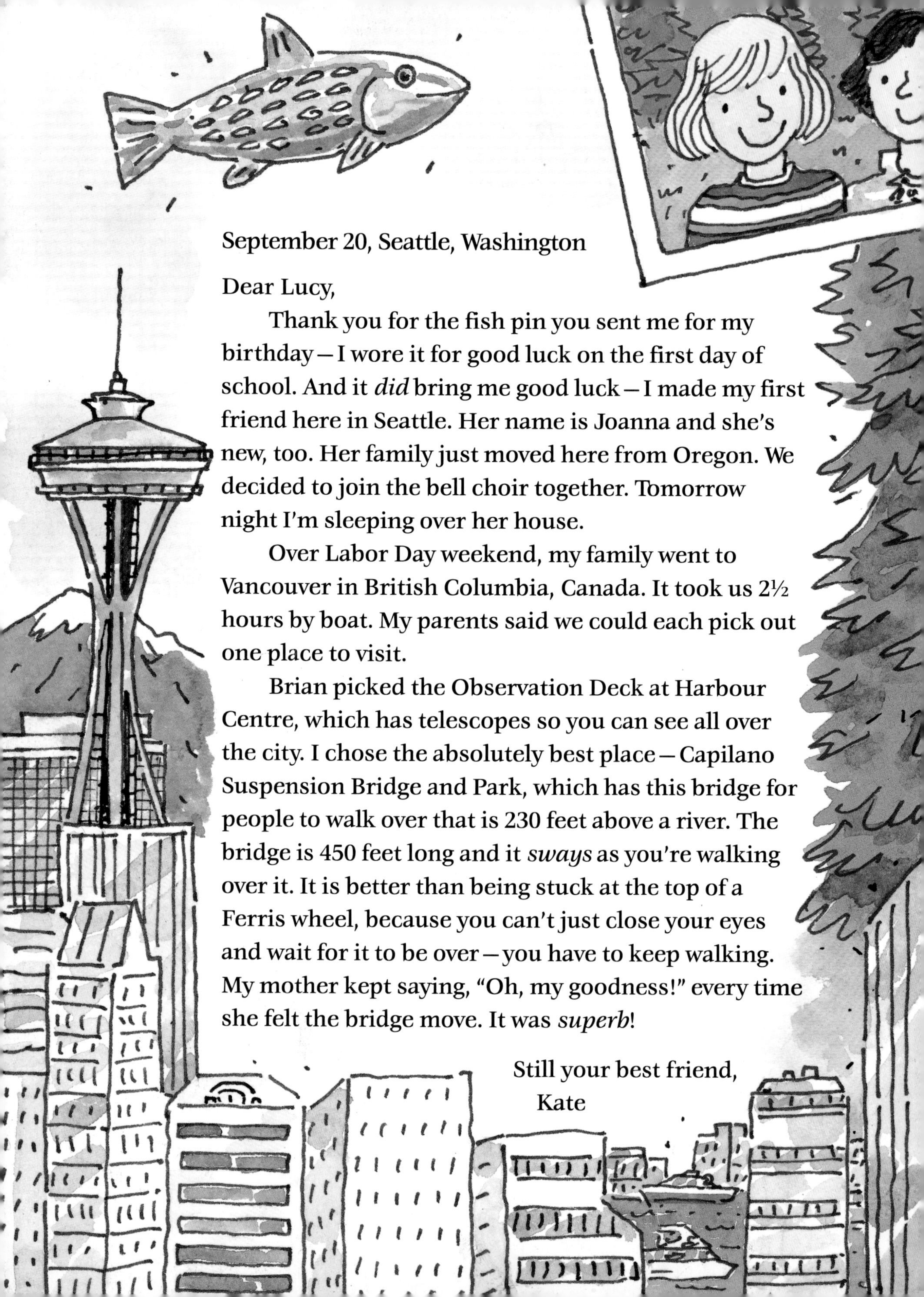

September 20, Seattle, Washington

Dear Lucy,

Thank you for the fish pin you sent me for my birthday—I wore it for good luck on the first day of school. And it *did* bring me good luck—I made my first friend here in Seattle. Her name is Joanna and she's new, too. Her family just moved here from Oregon. We decided to join the bell choir together. Tomorrow night I'm sleeping over her house.

Over Labor Day weekend, my family went to Vancouver in British Columbia, Canada. It took us 2½ hours by boat. My parents said we could each pick out one place to visit.

Brian picked the Observation Deck at Harbour Centre, which has telescopes so you can see all over the city. I chose the absolutely best place—Capilano Suspension Bridge and Park, which has this bridge for people to walk over that is 230 feet above a river. The bridge is 450 feet long and it *sways* as you're walking over it. It is better than being stuck at the top of a Ferris wheel, because you can't just close your eyes and wait for it to be over—you have to keep walking. My mother kept saying, "Oh, my goodness!" every time she felt the bridge move. It was *superb*!

Still your best friend,
Kate

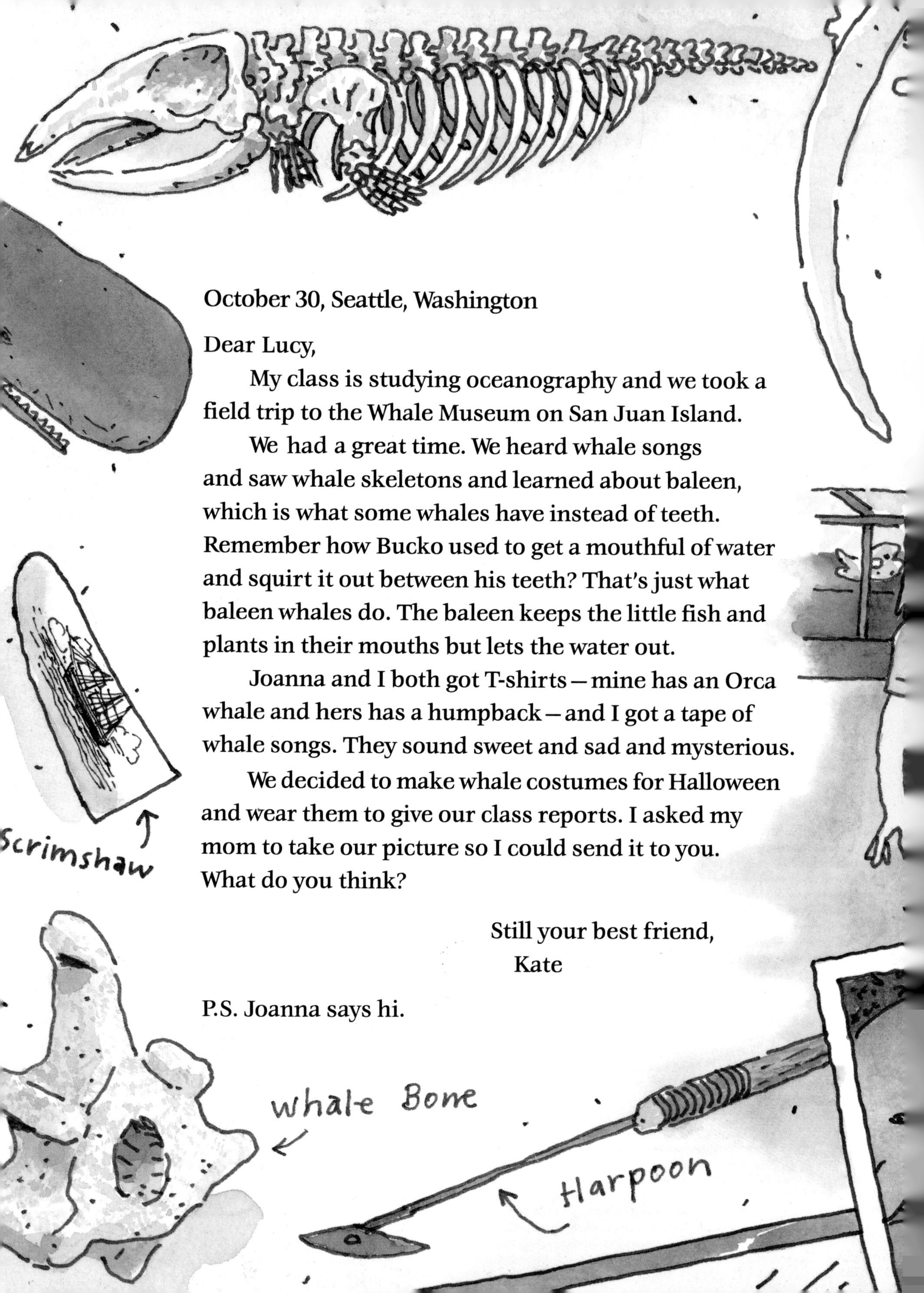

October 30, Seattle, Washington

Dear Lucy,

My class is studying oceanography and we took a field trip to the Whale Museum on San Juan Island.

We had a great time. We heard whale songs and saw whale skeletons and learned about baleen, which is what some whales have instead of teeth. Remember how Bucko used to get a mouthful of water and squirt it out between his teeth? That's just what baleen whales do. The baleen keeps the little fish and plants in their mouths but lets the water out.

Joanna and I both got T-shirts — mine has an Orca whale and hers has a humpback — and I got a tape of whale songs. They sound sweet and sad and mysterious.

We decided to make whale costumes for Halloween and wear them to give our class reports. I asked my mom to take our picture so I could send it to you. What do you think?

Still your best friend,
Kate

P.S. Joanna says hi.

41
MUSEUM

November 30, Hollywood, California

Dear Lucy,

I hope you had a good Thanksgiving. Mine was great! My parents said since all our relatives are back in New Jersey, there was no reason for us to stay home and eat turkey by ourselves, so we went to *Hollywood*! We saw the sidewalk with the names of all the stars, but we didn't see anyone famous.

We spent all of yesterday at Universal Studios. The scariest part was the simulated earthquake—it seemed so real. There were buildings falling apart and giant waves nearly drowning us and electric wires blazing and trucks practically crashing right into us.

Today we went to the Casa de Adobe—a nineteenth-century Spanish hacienda—and to El Pueblo de Los Angeles Historic Park. We saw exhibits about the people from Mexico who helped to settle this part of California. It reminded me of our trip to Mexico last year. But Brian isn't nearly as much fun to travel with as you are.

Still your best friend,
Kate

December 17, Seattle, Washington

Dear Lucy,

Merry Christmas! I hope you like your present. I got it for you when we went down to Portland, Oregon, to see the Winter Lights Festival. The Willamette River runs right through the middle of the city, and at Christmastime all the boats on it are outlined and decorated with lights. It's really pretty. But I think I liked the lights at the zoo even better. They have all these animal silhouettes made of lights. They make the lights go on and off, so it looks like the animals are moving.

Our holiday concert is tonight. My friend Joanna and I are both a little nervous. I wish you could be with us to hear how terrific we sound. Maybe someday…

Still your best friend,
Kate

January 26, Sumpter, Oregon

Dear Lucy,

Joanna invited me to go with her family to Oregon to see her Uncle Tom in the Elkhorn Crest Sled Dog Races. It took us almost eight hours to drive here. It was really cold (17°) and there was new snow and *lots* of dogs.

Joanna's uncle drove a six-dog sled (they call it "mushing") and the race was six miles long. We drank hot chocolate and cheered for him and his dogs, and they came in third. His dogs were so beautiful, and they were all named after towns in Alaska: Ketchikan, Juneau, Kodiak, Sitka, Fairbanks, and Umiat.

Remember that computer game about the Oregon Trail we played in Mrs. Snyder's class? The Oregon Trail went right by here and, at the National Historic Oregon Trail Interpretive Center, we saw a whole bunch of stuff that people really used on their trip—like frying pans and tools and some old parasols and diaries. There are still ruts in the ground from the wagon wheels—but there was too much snow for us to see them. And there were scenes of people making the trip—they all looked kind of dirty and worn out. I guess I would have been, too. Imagine going 2,000 miles with Brian in a wagon pulled by oxen. Yuck!

Still your best friend,
Kate

ELKHORN
A721

February 23, San Francisco, California

Dear Lucy,

My father had to go to a conference in San Francisco and, since it was during Chinese New Year, he said we should come along.

At the final parade there were lion dancers and pumpkin-headed lion teasers and *lots* of firecrackers, drums, and cymbals to scare away the evil spirits.

But the best thing was Gum Lung—the Golden Dragon—which was a block long and had twenty-two people inside holding it up and being the dragon feet. They made it slink along the street and moved its body like a wave. Its eyes were popping out of its head, it had horns and whiskers, and it was pink, blue, orange, and, of course, golden.

I'm sending you a Chinese yo-yo that I bought for you at the parade. It comes with a special Chinese New Year greeting: *Gung hay fat choy!* which means "May you prosper!"

Still your best friend,
Kate

P.S. We also rode on a cable car, went on a tour of Alcatraz Island, bought T-shirts with the Golden Gate Bridge on them, and took lots of pictures. How do you like them?

GOLDEN GATE
BRIDGE
ALCATRAZ

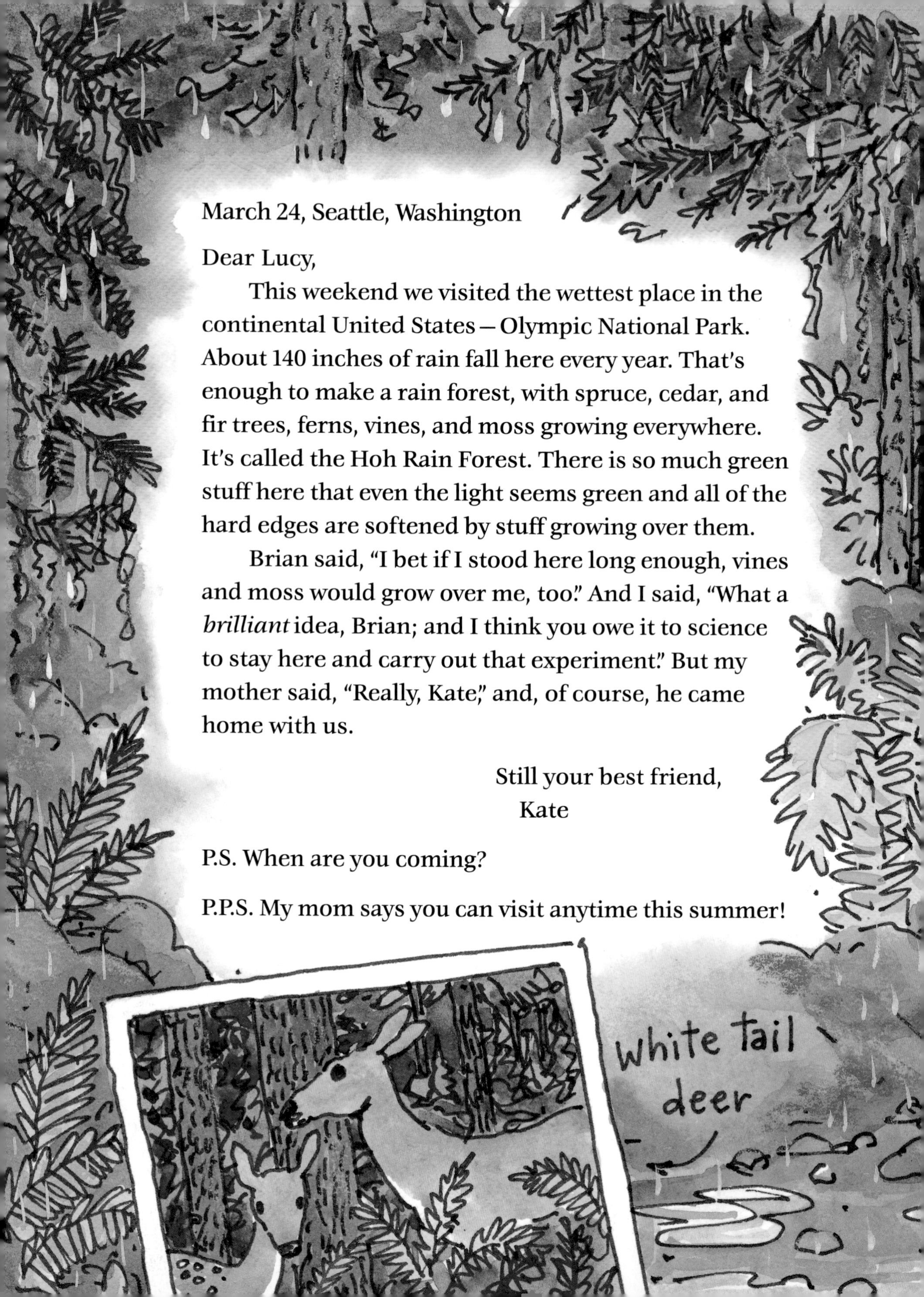

March 24, Seattle, Washington

Dear Lucy,

This weekend we visited the wettest place in the continental United States – Olympic National Park. About 140 inches of rain fall here every year. That's enough to make a rain forest, with spruce, cedar, and fir trees, ferns, vines, and moss growing everywhere. It's called the Hoh Rain Forest. There is so much green stuff here that even the light seems green and all of the hard edges are softened by stuff growing over them.

Brian said, "I bet if I stood here long enough, vines and moss would grow over me, too." And I said, "What a *brilliant* idea, Brian; and I think you owe it to science to stay here and carry out that experiment." But my mother said, "Really, Kate," and, of course, he came home with us.

Still your best friend,
Kate

P.S. When are you coming?

P.P.S. My mom says you can visit anytime this summer!

April 8, Honolulu, Hawaii

Dear Lucy,

Aloha from beautiful Hawaii! We're staying on the island of Oahu and we've been here five days so far. We've visited Makiki Forest, a pineapple plantation, and tomorrow we are going to Pearl Harbor.

Yesterday, we went to the Polynesian Cultural Center. There was a big outdoor pageant called "This is Polynesia," with volcanoes and waterfalls and fire walkers and hula dancers and over 100 people in the show. Plus, there were seven villages that each showed a different culture of the area. In the New Zealand village, I learned a Maori stick game called *tititorea,* and in the Tonga village, I made a palm frond headband. I'm even learning to do the hula!

Did you know that there are only twelve letters in the Hawaiian alphabet? (a,e,h,i,k,l,m,n,o,p,u, and w) Isn't that *great*—a language you can't even say "Brian" in.

Still your best friend,
Moana
(that's what I'll change my name to if I move to Hawaii. It means "ocean.")

P.S. Brian and I are going to take surfing lessons at Waikiki Beach!

May 24, Yosemite, California

Dear Lucy,

We're staying in tent cabins at Yosemite National Park for a few days and we're having a great time. We went on a tram tour of the Mariposa Grove of giant sequoias and saw Grizzly Giant, which is 2,700 years old! We hiked one trail along Tioga Pass, right at the top of the Sierra Nevada, and could look down and see mountain peaks and meadows on one side and high desert on the other. Plus we saw Upper Yosemite Falls – one of the tallest waterfalls in the world. It was *gigantic*!

Over the weekend we went to the Jumping Frog Jubilee in Angels Camp. My mother said there was a famous story written about it by Mark Twain. There were a zillion frogs there, all trying to beat the record of 21 feet 5¾ inches set by Rosie the Ribiter. If you don't have a frog, you can borrow one, so Brian and I got to enter the contest. We didn't even come close to winning, but my frog went 6½ inches farther than Brian's. He got upset but I said, "I wouldn't have jumped for you either if you had named *me* Wart Head." I named *my* frog Cassandra.

Still your best friend,
Kate

JUMPING FROG JUBILEE

June 21 — Summer at last!
Reedsport, Oregon

Dear Lucy,

We're on a camping trip along the coast of Oregon. Today we went to Sea Lion Caves. You have to take an elevator down about 200 feet and then you stand behind big, heavy windows to look at the sea lions. Most of them are outside on rocks in the summer but some were in there barking and bellowing. I told Brian it sounded like him singing in the shower.

We're staying at a campground at the Oregon Dunes National Recreation Area. The sand dunes there are almost like mountains and yesterday we rented off-road vehicles to explore a little. The dunes go for miles and miles.

We also saw about 100 elk grazing not far from here and went to this place called Devil's Churn. When the tide comes in, it rushes through a slit in this one rock. When it gets to the end of the slit, it bursts into the air like an explosion. It was spectacular!

Still your best friend,
Kate

July 6, Seattle, Washington

Dear Lucy,

I can hardly believe you'll be here in just a few days—I can't *wait.* You'll finally get to meet Joanna. We've been taking tennis lessons, and we'll teach you everything we've learned when you get here.

My father said we can all take a trip across Puget Sound to Winslow and fly kites from the ferry. (Brian's been asking to do that for *months.*)

My mother said if we can get up early enough we could go to Pike Place Market with her—she goes at the crack of dawn.

Plus, I want to show you my favorite statue ever and it's not in a museum—it's at a train station.

And Brian said if I'm extra nice to him he'll let you borrow his bike so we can ride on one of the trails. That shows you how glad I am that you're coming to visit—I'm even willing to be extra nice to Brian.

Still your best friend,
Kate

US MAIL
My favorite
statue

ALASKA
PACIFIC OCEAN
HAWAII
Seattle
WASH.
OREGON
CALIFORNIA